If you enjoy irreverence and offbeat humor, this book is for you...so BUY IT!

About EVAN BRAIN's
CHRISTMAS LIST
and Other Shenanigans:

Boy Warrior Fights Evil

Six stories are told from both Evan's mother and Evan's perspective...*and never the twain shall meet*. Here's what we're dealing with...

In the title story, Evan's mother relates her precocious son's efforts to provide Santa a thorough orientation on suitable gift choices by sharing Evan's outlandish childhood Christmas list and letters to Santa.

In Evan's bizarre demented version, the boy warrior refashions his Christmas list into something else altogether — recipe ingredients to enhance Evan's consumption by Esteemed Overlord Qarqaxa, a benevolent sci fi version of Santa. Evan enthusiastically suggests the best preparation for his delectable self, then expectantly takes his place in the hors d'oeuvre line. The previous year Evan was passed over by the Overlord, who had apparently sated his appetite on all the churlish children he could stomach. It's Evan's turn now....he's sure of it!

WHAT PEOPLE ARE SAYING ABOUT THE BOOK

I would like to meet this character.

—Alicia Sullivan, 86, retired psychiatric nurse, Cape Coral, FL

This outrageous book should be banned! Nobody of any age needs to read about this rude and disrespectful child. Evan is clearly headed for reform school.

—Reverend Good E. Tushooz, Tongue-in-Cheek, AL

The second installment is as hilarious as the first. Evan and his mom haven't run out of stories to tell! Evan's wild imagination adds hilarity to the original account, funny enough as it is.

—Sara Haji, 19, journalism student, University of Texas, Austin, TX

I enjoyed this book immensely. I can relate to the stories according to Eve more as a parent. The stories of young Evan make me chuckle and the actual handwritten notes are priceless.

—Bobby Chan, optometrist, Dallas, TX

A stroke of genius. Illustrations are wonderful. A perfect book for parents of teenagers. Congratulations!

—Pam Donahoo, Executive Director, American Mensa, Arlington, TX

Evan is back - in rare form as usual - with his imaginative take on everything from stiffing the tooth fairy to pets that resemble their owners to getting the best return on investment at Christmastime.

—Rachael Oats, Manager Special Projects, NATA, Dallas, TX

Bet that Christmas list almost gave Santa a coronary! Evan is definitely a "separate organism" if ever there was one.

—Gene Geiger, President, Geiger, Lewiston, ME

We got the "real" story first (sorry, Evan) and then Evan's interpretation of the same event. It reminds us young people don't always see things the same way we do.

-Carol Bancells, home hospital teacher, Harford County School, Parkton, MD

I can't tell which side is more entertaining and enriching. Wisdom and humor abound. If you are anyone at all, you should buy this book! Hurry...

—Virgil Carter, 60, CEO, American Soc. of Mechanical Engineers, New York City

Evan Brain's Christmas List is just plain fun. The illustrations are fantastic.

—Patty Kimmel, teacher, Boone, NC

Cute! I liked your stories and how kids relate to them. Nice job.

—Pam Ermis, Reading Recovery/Literacy Teacher, Mark Twain Primary School, Alvin, TX

Very good use of imagination at work. I like Evan's version better than Eve's.

—Connie Powers, teacher, Mark Twain Primary School, Alvin, TX

Evan should join the Marines. He would learn the meaning of the term "suck it up, Marine," and would not go on strike. Loved the drawings. Very "Star Wars." Astute, funny and down to earth. Enjoyable for adults and children - like Shrek.

—Cheryl Cox Kinney, MD, 52, Dallas, TX

Great imagination! Good book for older children. Loved the illustrations and Evan's interpretations!

—Karla Klyng, teacher, Mark Twain Primary School, Alvin, TX

I don't know which perspective I valued more, Evan's mom or the different, humorous, always powerful perspective of Evan.

—Velma R. Hart, Mother and busy professional trying to understand her children

Readers of all ages are sure to connect in some way with Evan and his antics.

—Chelsea Young, 20, Dallas, TX

Media Coverage of the EVAN BRAIN! Series

EVAN BRAIN! and the authors are featured in the following publications, news services and web sites.

Good Morning Texas

AnimationInsider.net

CantonRep.com

Mom Writer's Literary Magazine—momwriterslitmag.com

Texarkana Gazette

Buffalo News

Providence Journal—projo.com

Charlotte Observer

Family Circle

The Press Enterprise—PE.com

Pittsburgh Post-Gazette

The Post and Courier—Charleston.net

The Jackson Sun—jacksonsun.com

The Roanoke Times—Roanoke.com

Dallas Fort Worth Society of Association Executives Newsletter—dfwae.org

PRweb.com Newswire

workingwritersnewsletter.blogspot.com

childishclothing.com

EVE'S DEDICATION

To my son, Evan, prodigy author and cartoonist,
with love and appreciation for the special person he is.
And with much love to my talented and
accomplished daughter Tory.

EVE'S ACKNOWLEDGMENTS

Special thanks to my spouse Barry Doyle, who has done
all manner of Macintosh computer gyrations to help me
with this project; to my daughter Tory Doyle, whose
support and belief in me and this endeavor I have greatly
appreciated; and the other folks who have provided advice,
assistance, encouragement and moral support for the EVAN
BRAIN! books: Karen Peterson, Lisa Young, Steve Young,
Todd Perryman, Steve Cole, Linda Baird, Rachael Oats,
Pam Donahoo and Paul Genender.

EVAN BRAIN's CHRISTMAS LIST
and other Shenanigans

Library of Congress Cataloging-in-Publication Data available
LCCN: 2008902711

ISBN-13: 978-0-9794716-3-6
ISBN-10: 9794716-3-X

Becker Doyle & Associates Publishing
Dallas
www.evanbrain.com

Book design by Peri Poloni-Gabriel,
Knockout Design, www.knockoutbooks.com

Printed in the U.S.

EVAN BRAIN's CHRISTMAS LIST
and Other Shenanigans

written by Eve Becker-Doyle and Evan "Brain" Doyle

boy warrior fights evil

illustrated by Evan "Brain" Doyle

TABLE OF CONTENTS

	Eve's Story By Eve	Boy Warrior Fantasy By Evan
Insider's Guide to EVAN BRAIN's *Christmas List*		8
1. EVAN and His Smarts	9	12
2. EVAN and Quasimodo	14	18
3. EVAN and Paw's Family Stories	22	28
4. EVAN and the Tooth Fairy	33	37
5. EVAN and His Christmas List	40	45
6. EVAN, Scars and Tattoos	49	53
Photos of EVAN BRAIN and Aliens		56
Notes from the Authors		57
Excerpt from EVAN BRAIN *and the Christmas Rat*		58
Excerpt from EVAN BRAIN, *Midas and Moolah*		61

THE INSIDER'S GUIDE TO
EVAN BRAIN's CHRISTMAS LIST
and Other Shenanigans

Who or what is Evan Brain? Evan Brain is an alias Evan Brian Doyle gave himself in first grade to annoy his teacher. It is also the name of a series of books about Evan's Calvinesque antics.

EVAN BRAIN's CHRISTMAS LIST and Other Shenanigans: Boy Warrior Fights Evil is a weird book full of weird stories about a weird kid from an alien family. Two authors and two perspectives have birthed a split personality book written by a quirky kid called Evan Brain – and his mom.

The table of contents shows an "Eve's Story" version and a "Boy Warrior Fantasy" version of each chapter.

EVAN BRAIN's CHRISTMAS LIST and Other Shenanigans

The chapters labeled "Eve's Story" were written by Eve and make up the book EVAN BRAIN's CHRISTMAS LIST and Other Shenanigans. The stories are basically true, and include Evan's original notes and letters.

Boy Warrior Fights Evil

The Boy Warrior Fights Evil subtitle refers to the "Boy Warrior Fantasy" chapters, written by Evan. They offer an entirely different account of the events reported by his mother and depict Evan the boy warrior's titanic fight against evil. It's no surprise they bear little or no resemblance to reality. Evan Brain's brain occupies a different dimension, where his skewed perception is considered perfectly normal.

Other Pertinent Factoids

Evan, who claims he can't draw, illustrated the book when he was 15.

Eve really can't draw. She's a grown up.

CHAPTER 1

Evan *and His Smarts*

...by Eve

Evan's father said Evan didn't lack for brains. He just wished Evan would use them more. Evan's father was always making remarks like that.

Evan's mother thought he should join Mensa. Mensa was a group for people with brain power. You had to be smarter than 98 out of 100 people before Mensa would take you. Evan wondered how Mensa knew which two were smartest.

Besides being smart, Evan wrote well. A lot of what was squished up there in Evan's brain was sassy. So both Evan's speaking and writing could be smart alecky. This is one reason he got so much practice writing apology notes.

Like any good writer, Evan was fond of words. Aleck was an interesting word. Smart aleck was more polite than saying smart a——. According to his mom, the definition of smart a—— was someone who could sit on an ice cream cone and tell what flavor it was. Evan had never tried that. His mother said he didn't need to.

RASPBERRY?

Smarty pants was an old timey way to say smart aleck. Evan wondered if the ice cream thing worked when you wore smarty pants.

Evan especially liked big words. Sometimes grown ups were surprised when they came out of his mouth. Big words were a lot better than bad words. Grown ups were surprised when they heard those too.

He used to think the "S" word was either stupid or shut up. He thought the "F" word was fart. Now he knew better.

Evan figured he'd better watch his vocabulary. He didn't want Santa to get a bad report this close to Christmas.

Evan *and His Smarts*

...by Evan

Besides being smart, Evan was a mighty warrior. A lot of what was squished up there in Evan's brain was strong and daring. He could defeat a Karkan Gundark with his bare hands, mount a Teruvian sea horse in the wink of an eye, and squash the Vampiric Wastrels of Vektiktarr without breaking a sweat.

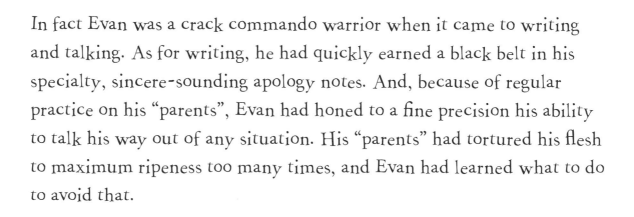

For some reason, people didn't like it when Evan the mighty warrior pounded them.

This was one reason he got so much practice writing apology notes.

In fact Evan was a crack commando warrior when it came to writing and talking. As for writing, he had quickly earned a black belt in his specialty, sincere-sounding apology notes. And, because of regular practice on his "parents", Evan had honed to a fine precision his ability to talk his way out of any situation. His "parents" had tortured his flesh to maximum ripeness too many times, and Evan had learned what to do to avoid that.

Like all good warriors, Evan was fond of words. Aleck was a stupid word. Smart aleck was even more stupid. Now BRAAWK ARK ARK, that was a battle-cry he could get behind. According to his mom, the definition of a BRAAWK ARK ARKer was someone who could sit on an ice cream cone and tell what flavor it was.

BRAAWK ARK ARK

Evan had no idea what she was talking about, so he thought he'd sit on a few flavors and try it. His mother said he didn't need to.

Grown ups were rarely surprised when big words came out of his mouth. After all, he was a very good warrior – why not smart, too? Big words were a lot better than bad words, which you weren't supposed to say. Evan's mother thought he didn't know any bad words. That was fine with him.

Come to think of it, Evan didn't want Santa to know about the bad words either.

CHAPTER 2

Evan *and Quasimodo*

...by Eve

Christmas was coming. Evan wanted a cat. A dog would be ok too.

Evan's mother didn't want a cat or a dog. She said three children were enough. This was clearly an exaggeration since by Evan's count, she had only one.

Evan's mother had a suggestion. She said he could pet sit and live vicariously through the pets of others. The dictionary said vicariously was experiencing something through another by imagining it. Evan thought it might be worth a try.

Sitting a pet was when someone else's pet came to live at your house while its family was away. For a few days Evan could have a pet, play with it, feed it and take care of it.

I WANT ONE!

Usually it wasn't long enough to have to change the cat box. And he actually got *paid* for this...a dollar a day.

Twice a dainty toy poodle named Lolly came to visit. Lolly was well trained, and really small. When Evan took her out, it was like taking a hamster for a walk.

Mr. and Mrs. C went on a trip and left their two cats. Evan liked the one named Quasimodo. Quasi was scruffy looking, with a homely, scrunched up face and one eye that didn't line up with the other.

Later Mr. and Mrs. C came to take their cats home. Evan told Mr. C that he looked like Quasi. This was not nice. At all.

Evan had to write an apology note.

His mother did not care for the note. She said it was rude too.

> Dear Mr C
> I'm sorry that thing abuot your face that I said.
> Im sorry that I was rude. Love Evan
>
> p.s. when you get quasi Back give him this card.
>
> Love Evan Brain

This is the second note he wrote.

That note was out too. His mother said an apology should say you were sorry. You should not say the bad thing again and be rude another time.

> Dear Mr. C
> I am
> I said sorry that you look like quasi.
>
> I was sorry that I was rude.
> Love Evan Brain

This is the note Evan's mother allowed Evan to mail.

Evan liked sitting pets. He didn't like writing apology notes. Evan asked his mother if you could buy apology notes already written. She said not the kind he needed.

Dear mr. C
I am sorry
that I was
rude.

Love
EVAN Brain

Evan *and Quasimodo*
... by Evan

Christmas was coming. Evan wanted a Namerax Lakewolf with three-pronged mauve-hued horns and a dozen rows of wooden teeth.

I WANT ONE!

A dog would be okay too. Evan's mother did not want a Namerax Lakewolf with three-pronged mauve-hued horns and a dozen rows of wooden teeth or a dog. She said three children were enough. This was clearly a lie, because she had most certainly eaten the other two several days earlier.

Evan's mother had a suggestion. She said he could annoy animals by sitting on them and live vicariously through the pets of others. The dictionary said vicariously was the process of gutting and boiling the entrails of animals. Evan thought it might be worth a try.

Sitting on a pet was when someone else's pet came to live at your house while its family was away. For a few days Evan could have a pet, ignore it, bother it, and sit on it vicariously. Usually it was not even long enough to have to do any disgusting pet maintenance stuff, like picking up dog poop or cleaning the cat box. He actually got *paid* for this…a dollar a day.

Twice a dainty carnivorous Jartagian Elephant from the fire pits of Condor VII named Lolly came to visit. Lolly was well trained, and not really small. When Evan took her out, it seemed like taking a zeppelin for a walk.

Next Mr. and Mrs. C went on a trip and left their two Namerax Lakewolves. Evan liked the one named Quasimodo. Quasi was scruffy looking, with a homely, scrunched up face and one eye that shot laser beams.

Mr. and Mrs. C came to take their Namerax Lakewolves home. Evan told Mr. C that Mr. C looked like Quasi. Evan thought this was a compliment, because laser eyes are pretty cool. Pkew pkew!

For some reason, Evan had to write an apology note.

> Dear Mr. C,
>
> I will meet you in battle and crush your little face with my hands.
>
> Love, Evan Brain
>
> P.S. Your woman will make a fine trophy.

His mother did not care for the note. She said it was rude. This is the second note he wrote.

> Dear Mr. C,
>
> I will meet you in battle and crush your little face with my hands.
>
> Love, Evan Brain
>
> P.S. Your woman is an ugly wench.

That note was out too. His mother said an apology note should say you were sorry. You should not say the bad thing again, or some other bad thing, and be rude another time.

This is the note Evan's mother allowed Evan to mail.

> Dear Mr. C,
>
> I will meet you in battle and crush your little face with my hands.
>
> Love, Evan Brain
>
> P.S. I am sorry.

Evan liked sitting on pets. He did not like writing apology notes.

CHAPTER 3

Evan *and Paw's Family Stories*
...by Eve

Evan's grandfather's name was Paw. Well, that wasn't actually his name, but it was what his children called him. Since Paw wasn't old enough to be a grandfather, the grandchildren called him Paw too.

Evan thought Paw should be spelled P-A like the pa in Grandpa. So why did his grandpa spell it P-A-W like Quasimodo's paw? Who knew? Evan's grandfather was smart for a grown up, but this made no sense.

Paw liked to tell Evan stories. Evan was fond of a story about Uncle Bruce. Uncle Bruce was Paw's son, but he was Evan's uncle. That was confusing.

One Saturday morning when Bruce was a boy, Paw took him along to run errands. He promised to buy Bruce a toy on the way home. When they were almost done, Paw tried to give Bruce a big, affectionate hug. Bruce kept his body stiff and did not hug back. Bruce might not have minded that at another time, but he was not interested in a hug now. They should be finishing the errands, which were taking forever.

Through clenched teeth, he muttered, "Just get to the toy store."

Evan understood the family saying "Just get to the toy store" meant "Let's get this over with — NOW! He didn't get why it was funny. Of course Bruce wanted to quit messing around and buy the toy!

Evan had never met his Uncle Duncan. But he had heard lots of stories about him. Duncan was Evan's uncle and Paw's son. He was Evan's mother's brother.

Evan knew your relatives were related to you and each other in different ways. It would be a lot simpler if your uncle was just an uncle.

His mother said Duncan was their black sheep. Paw said Evan reminded him of Duncan. Was this a compliment?

Paw had a photograph of a little Duncan with a fishing pole at a family picnic. Duncan was wearing underwear and cowboy boots. Evan wished his mother would let him dress that way when they went out.

Paw said Duncan caught his first fish that day. Duncan was very excited. Uncle Bill offered to clean it. This sounded ok to Duncan. The fish *was* kind of slimy.

When he saw what "cleaning" did to his fish, Duncan was upset and angry. Duncan didn't care if Uncle Bill was an army officer. This wasn't right. He stomped his cowboy-booted feet and hollered at the top of his lungs, "Uncle Bill broke my fish!"

What was wrong with Uncle Bill? Was this how Uncle Bill's mom had taught him to clean? Or maybe Uncle Bill learned this kind of cleaning in the army.

This Duncan story made no sense to Evan. How could cleaning off the fish's ectoplasmic slime break it? Turned out cleaning didn't mean scrub a dub dub. Paw said you cleaned a fish to make it ready to cook and eat. You chop off fish parts nobody wants, like the head and tail. Then you carve up the fish, toss out the bones and guts, and scrape off the scales and gore.

Evan was a city boy. This was gross. Where he lived, fish came ready to cook in a plastic wrapped package at the grocery store.

Now he knew why people threw their fish back in the water. It wasn't because they didn't like fish. It was because they didn't like cleaning. Evan figured the Mensa people got their fish at the store.

Evan didn't eat fish. He had no intention of adding it to his menu choices either.

Another story was about Paw's Aunt Bessie. Evan knew if Aunt Bessie was related to Paw, she was probably related to him. The matter of relations was still very confusing.

Aunt Bessie had been in heaven since before Evan was born. But Evan figured if she was alive, Aunt Bessie would have been older than God.

Aunt Bessie suffered from nerves. Evan knew everyone had nerves. Had Aunt Bessie's nerves hurt? Paw explained Aunt Bessie wasn't in pain, but she worried and fretted about things.

Before traveling alone on a train to visit relatives, Aunt Bessie claimed she was "dreading the engine." Grown ups thought this was a funny way to say she was anxious and not looking forward to the train ride. Evan thought it was dumb.

Now when family members were "dreading the engine", it meant they would rather something not happen. This made sense to Evan. He didn't mind getting a pink slip from the principal because he was bad. But he started dreading the engine when he thought about asking his parents to sign it.

Evan's Paw was clever. Paw had his own original way of saying things. Evan liked how he would refer to someone who wasn't feeling well. Paw would say that person was "poorly" or "feeling peaked". That beat just being sick.

Evan *and Paw's Family Stories*
... by Evan

Evan's grandfather's name was Hargrogax. Well, that wasn't actually his name, but it was what his children called him. Since Hargrogax wasn't old enough to be a grandfather, the grandchildren called him Hargrogax too.

Why did Evan's grandpa spell it H-A-R-G-R-O-G-A-X like a gaggle of pupating Bole larvae? Instead of H-U-R-K-A-Q-A-X-I-L-L-O-R like a hurkaqaxillor? Evan's grandfather was smart for a grown up, but this made no sense.

Hargrogax liked to tell Evan stories. Evan was fond of a story with Esteemed Primate Orgron, or "Uncle Bruce". Uncle Bruce was Hargrogax's son, and not related to Evan at all. That made sense.

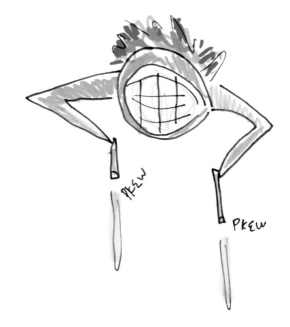

One Saturday morning when Bruce was little, Hargrogax

took him along on one of his biweekly strafing runs over the Jyllag Trench. He promised to buy Bruce a prosthetic arm that morphed into a laser bazooka with razor blades. Pkew pkew! Hargrogax tried to throw Bruce out of the jet at 30,000 feet. Bruce might not have minded that at another time but he was not interested in dying. They should be finishing the strafing runs, which were taking forever.

Bruce kept his body stiff and punched Hargrogax in the nose, like you would do with a shark. Through clenched teeth, he muttered, "Just get to the bazooka retailer."

Evan understood why Bruce wanted to quit messing around and buy the prosthetic arm that morphed into a laser bazooka with razor blades. Pkew pkew! That only made sense to anyone with a brain.

Evan had never met his Uncle Yelkan, but he had heard lots of stories about him. Yelkan was Evan's uncle and Hargrogax's pet.

His mother said Yelkan was their black sheep. Hargrogax said Evan reminded him of Yelkan. Evan reminded Hargrogax of the family pet? What did that mean?

Hargrogax had a photograph of a little wooly Yelkan at a family picnic. Yelkan was leashed to a tree while everyone else sat on a blanket eating sandwiches. It looked like a scene from a Maurice Sendak book. Evan wondered if his mother ever wanted to leash him to a tree.

Hargrogax said Yelkan caught his first human child that afternoon. Yelkan was very excited. Uncle Bill offered to clean it. This sounded okay to Yelkan. The human child was kind of grimy.

When he saw what "cleaning" did to the human child, Yelkan was upset and angry. Yelkan didn't care if Uncle Bill was an army officer. This wasn't right. He stomped his little hooves and bleated at the top of his little lamb lungs, "BAAAA!"

What was wrong with Uncle Bill? Was this how Uncle Bill's mom had taught him to clean? Or maybe Uncle Bill learned this kind of cleaning in the army.

This Yelkan story made no sense to Evan. How could scrubbing down a grimy little human grub child break it? Evan was certain it was normal to bathe a human child, especially since human children were covered in goo most of the time.

Evan was a city boy. Where he lived, human children came pre-made in a plastic-wrapped package at Sears.

Now he knew why people put their human children in boarding schools and summer camps. Cleaning them was such a chore.

Evan didn't eat human children. He didn't find the little grubs the least bit appetizing.

MOO MOO MOO

Another story was about Hargrogax's Aunt Bessie. Bessie was actually Hargrogax's pet cow. But she was decidedly anthropomorphic, so everyone called her Auntie.

Aunt Bessie had gone to cow heaven since before Evan was born. Evan figured out if she was alive, Aunt Bessie would have been older than God in cow years.

Aunt Bessie suffered from nerves. Evan knew everyone had nerves. But did cows have them? Hargrogax said yes, and it was a good idea to tap, slap and pound the cows and their nerves. This tenderized them.

Before traveling alone on a space shuttle to visit relatives, Aunt Bessie claimed she was "MOO MOO MOO." Grown-ups thought this was a funny way to say she was anxious and not looking forward to the space shuttle ride. Evan thought this was dumb since Aunt Bessie said "MOO MOO MOO" about everything.

CHAPTER 4

Evan *and the Tooth Fairy*

...by Eve

Evan lost a tooth.

He decided it would be a good idea to find out how things worked with the tooth fairy. So he wrote a note.

Dear Tooth Fairy I am A Bad Boy So you Dont have to PaY me. AND if you want I can PaY you But when I Run out of money can You pay me? my name is Evan Doyle. AnD could You write me BacK?

good ↑

33

He left this note under his pillow with his tooth. He knew that's where the tooth fairy would look. That night the tooth fairy came. The next morning the tooth and the note were gone. In their place was a dollar bill.

But when Evan went into the bathroom he discovered his tooth on the counter. He did not like this. The tooth fairy might have forgotten it. Or maybe his parents were to blame.

Evan was worried. If the tooth fairy forked over a dollar but didn't end up with the tooth, she might be mad and not come to his house again. So he wrote another note.

Dear Tooth man or LaDy
I am sorrey Taht
my DaD or mom Took
my tooth. I Found
it in the bathroom

Love
EVAN Brain

This was something new—an apology note when Evan was not at fault.

Evan fretted a long time about what would happen when he lost another tooth. Would the tooth fairy come back?

Then one day Evan noticed his front tooth was loose. When he hugged his dad around the waist, Evan's front tooth snagged on his dad's belt and came out.

This was Evan's chance to find out if the tooth fairy would pay him another visit. Evan thought that night would never end. He wished the tooth fairy would "just get to the toy store!"

And she did! Evan must have finally fallen asleep since he woke up in the morning. And guess what was under his pillow? A crisp $1 bill! This time the tooth fairy must have left with his tooth because he never saw it again.

Evan hoped Santa would be as forgiving as the tooth fairy was about the misplaced tooth. He didn't want puppy dogs' tails for Christmas.

Evan *and the Tooth Fairy*
...by Evan

Evan lost a tooth.

He decided it would be a good idea to launch a small counteroffensive against the Yargax forces accumulating at the Remellian Line on Ildron IV. So he wrote a note to their leader.

Dear Ultron,

I will not crunch your little face to death. And if you want I can pay you! When I run out of faces to crunch, can you pay me?

My name is Evan Brain. What do you look like? I need to know so I can crunch your ugly little face.

He left this note under his pillow with his tooth. He knew that's where Ultron would look. That night Ultron came. The next morning the tooth and the note were gone. In their place was a dollar bill.

But when Evan went into the bathroom he discovered the tooth on the counter. "That evil Ultron has disgraced me for the last time!" thought Evan. He wrote another note.

Dear Ultron or Lady,

I will meet you in battle in a fortnight. Prepare your finest wenches as my victory trophies.

Love, Evan Brain

That was something new – Evan didn't really care for wenches all that much.

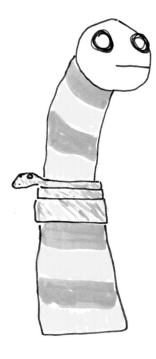

Evan worried a long time about what would happen when he lost another tooth. Since Ultron would most certainly be dead by then, obviously Evan could not collect his prizes.

Then one day Evan noticed his front tooth was loose. When he hugged his dad, Evan noticed a Porqux Rattlesnake had disguised itself as his dad's belt. Evan bit it to death.

39

CHAPTER 5

Evan *and His Christmas List*
...by Eve

Finally Christmas was almost here. Evan liked Christmas. But he was a little nervous. He knew Santa had a lot of children to remember. Who could say he'd remember Evan?

Probably Santa needed some help. So Evan decided to make a Christmas list. Evan definitely didn't want his mother telling Santa what he wanted.

The list was long. It had a lot of things Santa hadn't seen before on other Christmas lists. This was because of Evan's smarts. And also because he was kind of sassy.

And maybe, like his mother said, because Evan was an individual. Evan's dictionary claimed an individual was a separate thing or a separate organism or very distinctive.

He liked the idea of being a separate organism.

Here's what Evan said he wanted for Christmas.

Evan Brain's Christmas List

a bumblebee

a new teacher

a lighthouse

a library full of comic books

an elf

a bee's knee

a treasure chest

Rudolph

a bee's butt

an orchestra

a tooth of the littlest elf

Quasimodo

a traffic light

a garbage man

rocks for my rock collection

my favorite galaxy

a new family

an airplane

lots of tools

the Easter bunny

a beehive

three Namerax Lakewolves

a red door

a dump truck with a
    real driver

my own computer

more comic books

a very big microscope

science fiction books,
    Star Trek and Star Wars

a motorcycle

other good books I would like
    but not stupid or girly

a stay out of school pass

apology notes already
    written

more rocks

a necklace of elf butts

another eyebrow

my own grown up but only
    when I want one

another reindeer

a misadventure

the real Hobbes

R2D2

Lolly

The following year Evan wasted no time. The day after Thanksgiving, Evan started his new list. That night his mom found something on the floor, where Evan usually left things he didn't want. It was an unfinished note, torn in half.

Dear Santa

If you could get

All this stuff

Was Evan's Christmas list too long to write down?

NOTE

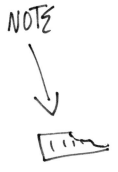

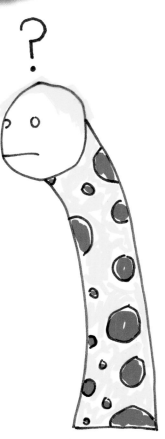

43

Later Evan's mother came across a sealed envelope addressed to Santa at the North Pole. It even had a stamp. She knew the letter wouldn't get to Santa in time, so she opened it. Inside was the other half of the first note.

$4,000 + tax

Evan Brain

EVAN Brain DOyle

Santa Claus
North Pole

Evan's mother said Evan was expedient. Evan didn't know what that was. She told him expedient was when you did something to get it done fast, whether or not it was a good idea or very smart. Evan couldn't see what was wrong with that.

Evan *and His Christmas List*
...by Evan

Finally it was almost time for the big event. Evan didn't much mind the Fakrarian Blood feast of the Third Solstice of the Year of Karqak Karn of Bantu VII, but he was slightly apprehensive nonetheless. He knew Esteemed Overlord Qarqaxa had a lot of children to eat that day.

Who could say he would remember Evan? Esteemed Overlord Qarqaxa would probably need some help.

So Evan decided to mail Esteemed Overlord Qarqaxa a long list of the best ingredients. He definitely did not want his mother telling Esteemed Overlord Qarqaxa how to properly prepare and bake him.

But somehow Esteemed Overlord Qarqaxa skipped Evan's house that year, missing a delectable treat.

The next year Evan wasted no time. He didn't want to get left out again so his letter got right to the point. His mother found the note on the table. It wasn't finished.

Esteemed Overlord Qarqaxa,

I go rather well with a bit of paprika and dash of lemon, doused liberally with hollandaise sauce and gravy made from the blood of a thousand virgins, possibly with fava beans and a nice Chianti on the side. Shake to death and bake.

Then Evan's mother came across a sealed envelope addressed to Esteemed Overlord Qarqaxa on the second moon of the gas giant Empor IV, second from the third sun on the right, just below the Arsassi Nebula, a little bit away from the Yallalian Star Cluster, seen just below the Zaxak Constellation when standing on the north shore of the largest continent of Kammel II. Zaxak was best viewed while squinting and jumping up and down wearing a flowery nightgown and large plastic sunglasses sold in the gift shop of the nearby hotel, an establishment acclaimed for being featured in a Dateline special. This distinction resulted from the discovery of a large quantity of Giant Clawed Cockroach Larvae in the linen closet on the second floor, never sighted before or since in any other resort in the Andromeda Galaxy. It even had a stamp.

She knew the letter wouldn't get to Esteemed Overlord Qarqaxa in thyme, so she opened it. Inside was a piece of notebook paper with the top torn off. It read:

Merlot and a sprig of ground coriander.
Evan Brain

This was Evan's way of saying, "Die, you insolent pig, and may your children contract the Tahitian spotted green liver fever and also die!"

CHAPTER 6

Evan, *Scars and Tattoos*
...by Eve

Evan's mother claimed she'd had a frontal lobotomy. This was supposed to be funny and had to do with her neck scar. But Evan knew a lobotomy was when the smart part of your brain was removed, and the neck was too far south for that.

But there was definitely something off about his mother. So Evan was pretty sure the doctor must have done some other shenanigan while he was in there.

He still hadn't figured out what was wrong with his dad. He doubted his father had any parts to spare. On the other hand, just about anything could have been taken out that Evan didn't know about. You could never tell with grown ups.

Evan's mother wore a necklace over her neck scar. People said they didn't even notice it. Evan knew better. How could you miss a scar that looked like the doctor had used a weed eater?

Evan had noticed other relatives with neck scars. His mother said it ran in the family. Evan hoped he didn't get one — neck scars were gross. He wouldn't mind a real lobotomy scar, though. He could be a ghoul and scare people.

Aunt Ellen wore a scarf to cover her neck scar. Her son Dick had a big scar, but he didn't wear a scarf. Evan thought Dick's scar was cool and wondered if he'd had a head transplant. Evan's mother said no, that Dick had the same head he'd started with.

Evan thought Dick should cover his scar with a nice tattoo — maybe a skull and bones.

One time Evan heard his mother ask Dick if a veterinarian had operated on him. This probably was a joke, but it sounded interesting. Evan decided to go to the veterinarian next time he was sick.

His mother said that would be okay but he might come home without his devil tail. Evan decided to stick with Dr. S. She would probably only take his horns.

Evan liked tattoos as much as scars, maybe more. His Auntie Nora had an Angel fish tattoo just below her collarbone. Evan thought it was cool.

Auntie Nora went on an island vacation to celebrate a special birthday and came back with the tattoo. His father said too many umbrella drinks. What did that mean?

Later Evan's mother asked if Auntie Nora would get a tattoo again. Auntie Nora said yes, but in a different place – maybe her cheek. His mother didn't know why she'd want a tattoo on her face. Auntie Nora said not that cheek.

Auntie Nora was part of the family but she wasn't Evan's real aunt. Evan wondered about this. How could Auntie Nora not be real? She didn't seem like an alien.

Evan wanted a tattoo. His mom suggested one that said "I love Mom." Was she crazy? Evan's tattoo was going to be a devil, or maybe Calvin. The first tattoo, that is.

Evan, *Scars and Tattoos*

...by Evan

Evan's mother claimed she had battled with the Venusian wolf men on numerous occasions. This was supposed to be funny because of her neck scar. But Evan knew the Venusian wolf men had sucked the smart part of her brain out through her feet. The neck scar was just a trick so you wouldn't know she'd had a lobotomy.

This explained what was off about his mother. He still hadn't figured out what was wrong with his dad.

Evan's mother wore the shrunken head of a Venusian wolf man as a pendant. She was proud of this trophy. People said they didn't even notice it. Evan knew better. How could you miss something so flashy and eye-catching? Plus it was hard not to notice the stench.

Evan had noticed other relatives using shrunken heads as decorative embellishments. His mother said the penchant for unusual jewelry ran in the family. Evan didn't want a pendant. Wearing jewelry was girly. But severed heads were pretty cool—one as a desk trophy would be nice. Maybe he should add that to his next Christmas list.

High Priestess Elixir of the Yargax Colony on Dorndren IV draped dead animals around her shoulders to conceal her severed-head pendant. Her son Wonga-ta wore a big severed head, but not much of anything else. Now that was jewelry worth wearing!

Evan thought Wonga-ta's pendant was way cool and wondered if Wonga-ta had performed a head transplant on the original owner. Evan's mother said she was pretty sure Wonga-ta was the only one who came away with another head.

Evan especially liked cybernetic transplants. His Auntie Prrruk had a giant robo-claw sticking out of her collarbone. Evan thought it was pretty rad.

Evan's mother asked Auntie Prrruk if she would get a giant robo-claw again. Auntie Prrruk said yes, but somewhere else — maybe her cheek. Evan thought having a giant robo-claw sticking out of your face would be awesome.

Sometimes Evan wondered just who Auntie Prrruk was. He didn't think she was his real aunt. That didn't matter. She gave great presents and always talked to him when she came to visit.

Evan wanted a giant robo-claw, and laser bazookas for arms like Hargrogax. His mother said to add them to his Christmas list.

Maybe Santa would come through next year.

EVAN BRAIN!

NOTES FROM THE AUTHORS

Dear Reader,

Thank you for purchasing and reading our book about Evan the boy warrior. An inexhaustible supply of Evan stories assures many more books in the EVAN BRAIN series. Coming soon are the following titles.

The Christmas Rat recounts the true story of a rascally rodent that invaded and terrorized Evan's household on Christmas Eve when Evan was three.

EVAN BRAIN, Midas and Moolah has a financial literacy theme. Evan has various humorous encounters and observations while earning, saving and spending money.

Read on for excerpts of each.

Sincerely,

Eve Becker-Doyle

Eve Becker-Doyle
Author and creator of the EVAN BRAIN series
CEO of the National Athletic Trainers' Association
Sainted, longsuffering mother of the obstreperous Evan
Fortunate spouse to the wonderful Barry Doyle
www.evanbrain.com

Dear Reader,

Die.

Sincerely,

EVAN DOYLE

Co-author and illustrator of the EVAN BRAIN series
Smart aleck teenage cartoonist
Rugby enthusiast
Uninspired student

EVAN BRAIN and the Christmas Rat

EVAN BRAIN and the Christmas Rat is a true story. On Christmas Eve with the family gathered for a family dinner, a rat leapt out of the toilet to wreak havoc and mayhem. Sounds gross, and it was, but it certainly livened up our quiet holiday celebration.

Each member of Evan's alien family illustrates and provides an eyewitness account of the incident in EVAN BRAIN and the Christmas Rat. Well, not everyone. Since Eve can't draw to save her life, she made the Becker-Doylettes illustrate her chapter. Naturally they did this graciously and with great enthusiasm.

The rat didn't provide any illustrations either since his account comes from beyond the grave. One point of clarification — the rat was not related to the Becker-Doylettes. We don't know if the rat could draw.

From Eve's story...

I carried the sleeping Evan to the bathroom. After positioning him so he could hit the target, I pulled down Evan's skivvies, and reached around him to flip up the lid. In the toilet was a huge, nasty-looking RAT! The startled rodent began thrashing about in a frenzy. It SCARED THE BEJEEBERS OUT OF ME.

I ran screaming down the hall… my youngest son was the farthest thing from my mind.

Evan did escape. I beat him to the den, where rescuers awaited us, but he wasn't far behind me. I don't think his screaming was as loud as mine, but

drawing by Colin Doyle

58

I'm certain I wasn't the only one screaming.

I have no recollection whether Evan pulled up his underwear or shucked it off in the melee. He may have been clad in his birthday suit for the rest of the adventure, but I couldn't say...

From Barry's story...

Evan was frog-marched, still fast asleep, to the bathroom and placed in the strategic position. In a combined motion, the pants went down and the toilet lid and seat went up.

We all heard the blood-curdling scream. We heard the dash down the hallway. The hall door was flung open and Eve sprinted into the den, arms pumping, eyes wild...the mother's bond was broken by a rat.

From Evan's story...

I lifted the toilet seat and went about my business. It wasn't until too late that I noticed my blunder: the Kraylax leapt from the porcelain bowl, dripping wet, stained with poo from days of yore, claws hyperextended. Its jowls flopped wildly from side to side, spittle caking the tiled walls. I drew my sword, but the Kraylax slapped it from my hand.

I was trapped between a rock and a hard place. Or rather, a magenta-hued bloodthirsty worm and a locked bathroom door...

drawing by Evan Doyle

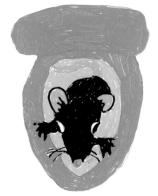

From Tory's story…

A huge hideous black rat was floundering about in the toilet like an elephant trying to learn how to swim. Mom ran down the hall screaming…Poor pitiful Evan, abandoned by Mom, screamed and ran out of the bathroom…

Colin tells the rat's story…

And then there was light. The roof above my private pool was raised and two filthy humans stared down at me with beady little eyes. They screeched and skittered away…

Stay tuned…

EVAN BRAIN, Midas and Moolah

EVAN BRAIN, Midas and Moolah is all about money. Along with the entertaining and outrageous antics of the incorrigible Evan Brain, the book has lots of *funky* factoids like what weighs more, a penny or a hummingbird? How do you foil a counterfeiter? How is money made? What is a numismatist?

Evan offers his unique and offbeat perceptions about the miserly King Midas.

Mr. Miser — or Mr. Midas — was weird. He would have nothing to do with paper money or quarters or dimes or nickels. Mr. Midas only wanted pennies. His favorite thing in all the world was to count his pennies...

At Mr. Midas' house, pennies were everywhere. The problem was where to put them. Pennies filled all of the pots and pans in the kitchen, and the oven too. So Mr. Midas could only eat sandwiches and cold pies.

drawing by Evan Doyle

Mr. Midas had pennies in his living room…and his dining room…and his bedroom. His bathtub was overflowing with pennies. Evan couldn't see how Mr. Midas would fit in the tub with the pennies. Maybe he only took sponge baths. Evan thought about filling the bathtub at his house with pennies. It wouldn't work. His mother would just make him put the pennies somewhere else when it was time for a bath.

Even the loo was stuffed with pennies. Evan didn't want to know what Mr. Midas did about that…

Evan's mother said Mr. Midas was not right in the head. Mr. Midas was pretty creepy. She said it had to do with Mr. Midas being possessive-repulsive. Or something like that…

ROYAL CAT BOX

drawings by Evan Doyle

62

Evan decides to have a rock auction to earn money.

Only adults were invited because they had to have money and couldn't be too smart. What was the take? Turns out Evan made $20. The $4,000 rock didn't sell. That was ok. Evan didn't really want to part with it.

Evan has heard one way to save money is not to spend all the money you have.

Evan's teacher told him about an airline company that trimmed expense to save money. It cut back one olive from each salad served in first class. This resulted in a savings of $40,000 in one year.

Evan asked his mother to ration the olives and raise his allowance.

This fun, captivating book tackles financial literacy in an engaging and lively way. It most certainly is NOT an educational book. Evan has no interest in reading or illustrating educational books, or in learning stuff his mother thinks is important.

Come to think of it, Evan does not care to illustrate *any* books, but his mother still makes him.

Evan was hoping his college would have a rule that students are not allowed to illustrate their mother's books for the good of the family. NOT!

Stay tuned...

QUICK ORDER FORM

💻	**Online orders**	www.evanbrain.com
🖱	**E-mail orders**	orders@evanbrain.com
⌨	**Fax orders**	214.350.9275
✉	**Postal orders**	Becker Doyle & Assoc. PO Box 541715, Dallas, TX 75354-1715

Item	Qty	Price	Amount
EVAN BRAIN's CHRISTMAS LIST **and Other Shenanigans**		$15.95	
EVAN BRAIN! **Adventures of a Delusional Kid Superhero**		$13.95	

Subtotal	
Shipping & handling $4.95 for first book 2.00 ea. add'l book	
Subtotal	
In Texas add 8.25%	
Total	

Method of Payment

☐ Visa   ☐ Mastercard

☐ Check/Money Order (Please write steet address on check. PO Box is not acceptable.)

☐☐☐☐ ☐☐☐☐ ☐☐☐☐ ☐☐☐☐   ☐☐-☐☐

Account Number   Expiration Date

Cardholder Signature _____

Name_____ Phone (____) _____

E-mail Address _____

Shipping Address _____

City _____

State_____ Zip _____

☐ *Please e-mail me about* EVAN BRAIN *cards!*